THE FOX WITH COLD FEET

To librarians, parents, and teachers:

The Fox with Cold Feet is a Parents Magazine READ ALOUD Original — one title in a series of colorfully illustrated and fun-to-read stories that young readers will be sure to come back to time and time again.

Now, in this special school and library edition of *The Fox with Cold Feet,* adults have an even greater opportunity to increase children's responsiveness to reading and learning — and to have fun every step of the way.

When you finish this story, check the special section at the back of the book. There you will find games, projects, things to talk about, and other educational activities designed to make reading enjoyable by giving children and adults a chance to play together, work together, and talk over the story they have just read.

The Fox
with Cold Feet

by Bill Singer

pictures by
Dennis Kendrick

Gareth Stevens Publishing • Milwaukee
Parents Magazine Press • New York

For a free color catalog describing Gareth Stevens' list of high-quality books, call 1-800-341-3569 (USA) or 1-800-461-9120 (Canada).

Parents Magazine READ ALOUD Originals:

Golly Gump Swallowed a Fly
The Housekeeper's Dog
Who Put the Pepper in the Pot?
Those Terrible Toy-Breakers
The Ghost in Dobbs Diner
The Biggest Shadow in the Zoo
The Old Man and the Afternoon Cat
Septimus Bean and His Amazing Machine
Sherlock Chick's First Case
A Garden for Miss Mouse
Witches Four
Bread and Honey

Pigs in the House
Milk and Cookies
But No Elephants
No Carrots for Harry!
Snow Lion
Henry's Awful Mistake
The Fox with Cold Feet
Get Well, Clown-Arounds!
Pets I Wouldn't Pick
Sherlock Chick and the Giant
    Egg Mystery

Library of Congress Cataloging-in-Publication Data

Singer, Bill.
    The fox with cold feet / by William Singer ; pictures by Dennis Kendrick. — North American library ed.
        p. cm. — (Parents magazine read aloud original)
        Summary: Wanting to protect his feet from the snow, Fox collects an odd assortment of make-shift boots from his animal friends in return for doing them favors, but just who benefits most is questionable.
    ISBN 0-8368-0890-8
    [1. Boots—Fiction. 2. Foxes—Fiction. 3. Animals—Fiction.] I. Kendrick, Dennis, ill. II. Title. III. Series.
    PZ7.S6157Fo 1993
    [E]—dc20   92-27113

This North American library edition published in 1992 by Gareth Stevens Publishing, 1555 North RiverCenter Drive, Suite 201, Milwaukee, Wisconsin 53212, USA, under an arrangement with Parents Magazine Press, New York.

Text © 1980 by William Singer. Illustrations © 1980 by Dennis Kendrick. End matter © 1992 by Gruner + Jahr, USA, Publishing/Gareth Stevens, Inc.

Printed in the United States of America

1 2 3 4 5 6 7 8 9 98 97 96 95 94 93

One crisp morning young Fox
leaped out of his den.
A thick blanket of snow
covered the ground.

Just then, Sparrow flew by, looking for seeds.

Fox was pleased with himself.
He sang an old fox song:

Fox followed Sparrow to the
bare elm tree where she lived.

Tree trunk.
Dig, dig.
Boot there.

All I have found are some seeds.

Good, good.

Good seeds.

11

She tugged at an empty nest,
and it fell to the ground.

CRUNCH!   CRUNCH!

Fox tried to run,
but he couldn't.
So he slowly made his way
uphill and downhill until
he came to a frozen pond.
Beaver was adding branches
to his dam.

Why does a Fox need boots?

Sparrow said they would keep my feet warm. So after I dug up the seeds for her, she gave me this boot.

Okey dokey. Bring those handy dandy branches over here. Under the good wood is a boot.

So young Fox carried
branch after branch.
He kept looking
for a boot under the wood.
But he didn't see one.
Finally, he brought the last
branch to Beaver.

But it seemed better than nothing.
And Fox went off to see if Raccoon could help him.

Fox slipped and slid through the snow.
At last he came to a hollow tree.

Soon Raccoon peeked
out of the hollow tree.

So, it's the clever young Fox.

You woke me from
my midwinter nap.

I'm sorry to bother you,
but I'm looking for
two more boots.

24

Raccoon slowly stepped out of the hollow tree and dragged himself through the forest.

Fox followed, slipping and sliding in the snow.
At last they came to an old campsite.

28

So Fox pushed...

and pulled...

and pushed.

At last the garbage can fell over.
Then he pulled the lid off.

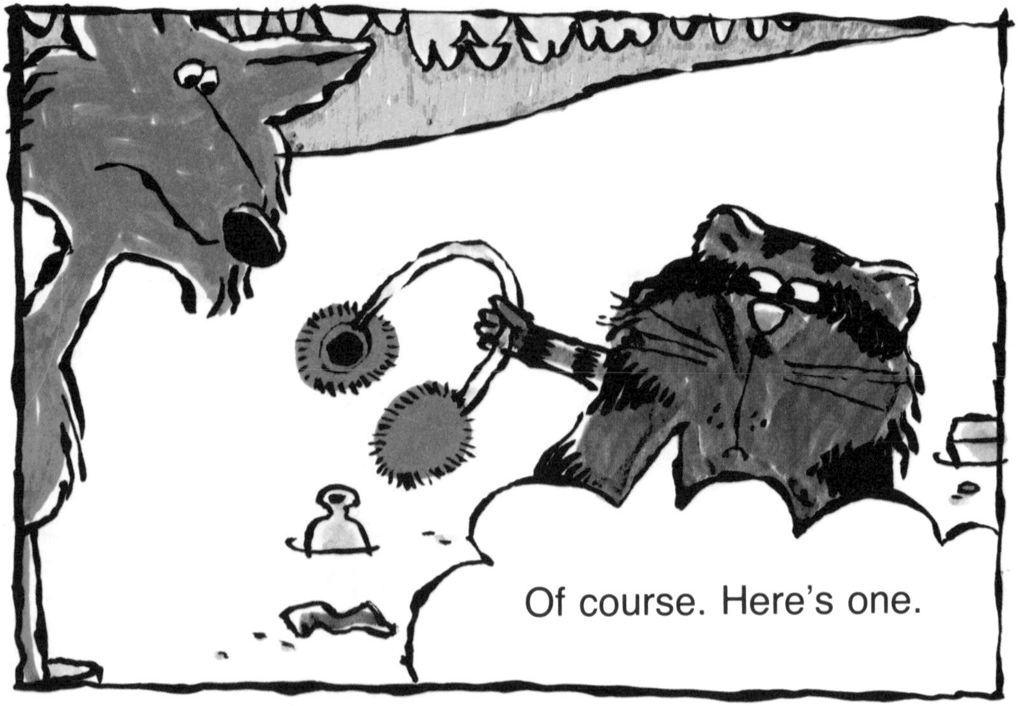
Of course. Here's one.

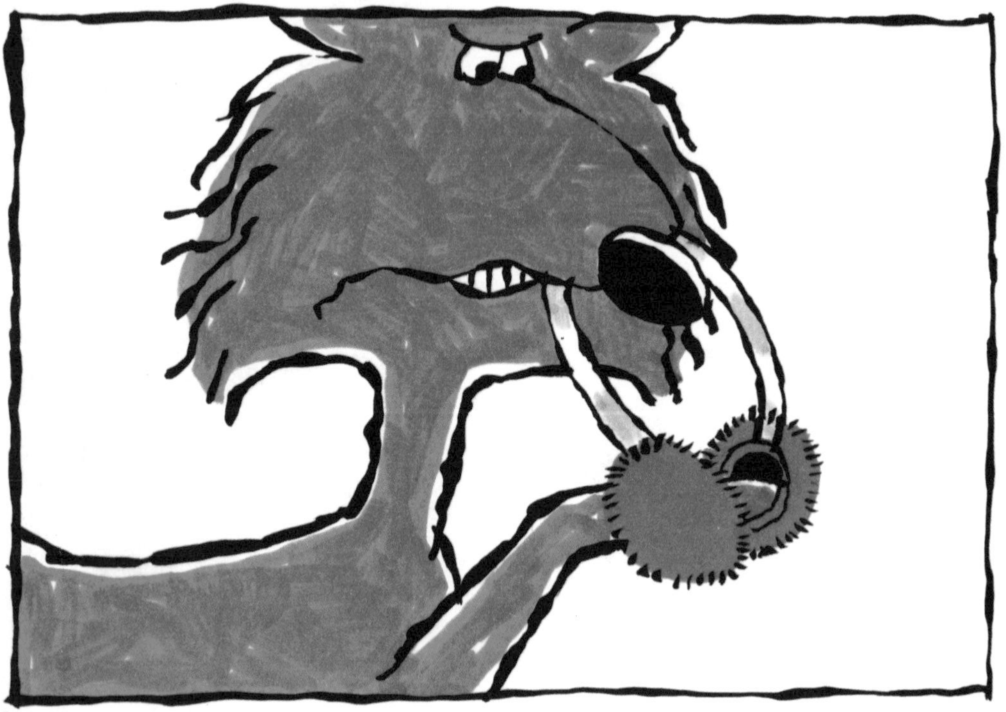

CRUNCH! CLUNK! THUD! THUNK!

PLOP!

Take your time.
Get used to your new boots.

CRUNCH! CLUNK! THUD! THUNK!

PLOP!

I'll take the pail off, too.
Maybe then I can walk faster.

THUD!　　THUNK!

PLOP!

Aha! I know what to do.

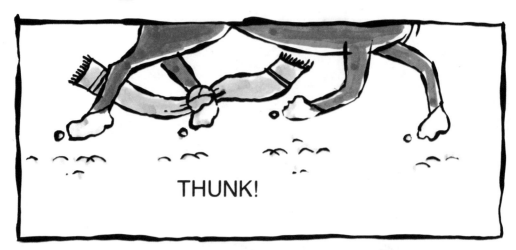

THUNK!

PLOP!

43

Fox ran all the way back
to his den, never
tripping, slipping, sliding, or falling.

And at last
Fox was right.

Notes to Grown-ups

Major Themes

Here is a quick guide to some major themes and concepts at work in *The Fox with Cold Feet:*

- Human nature: how easy it is to be taken advantage of by others
- The importance of doing what *you* think is right for yourself

Step-by-step Ideas for Reading and Talking

Here are some ideas for further give-and-take between grown-ups and children. The following topics encourage creative discussion of *The Fox with Cold Feet* and invite the kind of open-ended response that is consistent with many approaches to reading, including Whole Language:

- Take a close look at some of Fox's different facial expressions. For example, compare his expressions on pages 9, 22, 24, and 44-45. Discuss how these different expressions reflect his moods and feelings of self-confidence.
- Do the same for the other animals. Ask how we know what these animals think about Fox just from looking at their faces.
- Fox is a trusting soul, and like many children, he may not be able to tell the difference between good and bad advice. Ask kids to make up stories about other situations in which some people might take advantage of them. Encourage them to talk about how important it is to think for themselves and to be careful of trusting the wrong people.

Games for Learning

Games and activities can stimulate young readers and listeners alike to find out more about words, numbers, and ideas. Here are more ideas for turning learning into fun:

Experimenting with Patterns

"Crunch, clunk, thud, thunk, PLOP! Crunch, clunk, thud, thunk, PLOP!" The fox with cold feet walks his pattern into the snow.

Recognizing patterns, both auditorally and visually, is an essential skill children need in order to learn to read. Matching colors and shapes that are the same, tracking from left to right, and noting the order in which letters occur are all part of learning to recognize the patterns that form written words.

Stringing necklaces with patterns of large and small, or arranging colors repeated in a regular manner, are ways your child can begin to experiment with patterns. Because a necklace string is linear, your child will actually be making a color "sentence," while she or he also creates a necklace to wear. And chanting the pattern as you work together (red-red-*blue,* red-red-*blue,* for instance) can help reinforce the pattern auditorally as you go along.

You will need two long shoelaces (one for you and one for your child), or two pieces of string with ends wrapped tightly in tape to make a firm "needle" end.

You can make lots of fun necklaces from these household materials:

- cereals with O-shapes, especially fruit-covered ones;
- macaroni and colored pasta;
- plastic beads of varying colors and/or sizes.

Another way to help your child experiment with patterns is to glue cereals, pasta, or even dried beans and peas into pattern "sentences" on stiff paper. White glue will hold most shapes well. Cereal, bean, and pasta patterns also make great frames for your child's drawings.